With Love from Daniel

by Patty Michaels

poses and layouts by Jason Fruchter

Ready-to-Read

Simon Spotlight

New York   London   Toronto   Sydney   New Delhi

SIMON SPOTLIGHT
An imprint of Simon & Schuster Children's Publishing Division
1230 Avenue of the Americas, New York, New York 10020
This Simon Spotlight edition December 2023
© 2023 The Fred Rogers Company
For information about special discounts for bulk purchases, please contact
Simon & Schuster Special Sales at 1-866-506-1949 or business@simonandschuster.com.
Manufactured in the United States of America 1023 LAK
2 4 6 8 10 9 7 5 3 1
ISBN 978-1-6659-4246-1 (hc)
ISBN 978-1-6659-4245-4 (pbk)
ISBN 978-1-6659-4247-8 (ebook)

I really like
spending time
with Jodi.

We like to color
and draw together.

Katerina and I love to play with stuffies.

I love playing pretend with Miss Elaina.

I really like helping my mom make breakfast.

I love Circle Time with Teacher Harriet.

Going to the market
with my dad
is the best!

I love playing together at Jungle Beach.

I love to cuddle
with Tigey.

Playing explorers with
Prince Wednesday
is so fun!

I really love to read books with O the Owl.

Bath time
with Margaret
is always fun!

I love it when Music Man Stan plays his guitar!

I love my friends and family, and I love you, too, neighbor!

ABRAHAM LINCOLN

by Kristin Cashore

PEARSON

Scott
Foresman

Editorial Offices: Glenview, Illinois • Parsippany, New Jersey • New York, New York
Sales Offices: Needham, Massachusetts • Duluth, Georgia • Glenview, Illinois
Coppell, Texas • Sacramento, California • Mesa, Arizona

In 1860 people did not agree about slavery. Slavery was not allowed in the North. Slavery was allowed in the South. **Enslaved** people did not get paid. Their food and **shelter** were not good.

These people escaped slavery and came to the North.

Abraham Lincoln became President.
Lincoln thought slavery was wrong.

This is a poster from 1860.

Some of the southern states broke away.
Abraham Lincoln thought the states
should work together.

President Lincoln takes office.

Many people in the South wanted **independence** from the rest of the country. War broke out between the North and the South.

Lincoln visited battlefield camps during the Civil War.

The North won the war.
The South became part of the United States again.
Slavery in the United States ended.

President Lincoln was killed soon after the war was over.

Thanks to Lincoln our country stayed together. Now Americans try to work together just as Abraham Lincoln showed us.

Glossary

enslaved made to live as slaves, or owned as property

independence to be free from other people or places

shelter a place where people live